Hannah Savannah just _has_ to find the key to the carriage house for Mama!

Meet Hannah Savannah. This energetic and determined ten-year-old hopes to solve a mystery… with the help of her very best friends, Eduardo and Tiesha.

However, Eduardo is "chicken scared" of the ghost seen in a building behind Hannah's row home.

Tiesha prefers paper cutting and Origami to finding old keys.

Summer vacation is here and Hannah needs _help_ with her spying.

Ten is boring.

Make-up is gross.

Little brothers whine a lot.

However, being a **super spy** is absolutely the best thing on earth!

Carriage House
Key

Hannah Savannah Finds
The Missing Key

Written & Illustrated
By

Pamela Munson Steadman

Published by Pamela Munson Steadman
Savannah, Georgia

Hannah Savannah Series

Book One

ISBN: 1-59196-101-7

Printed in the US by InstantPublisher.com

About the Author

Pamela Munson Steadman lives in her favorite city, Savannah, Georgia with her husband, Wayne.

When she is not writing, Pam is out telling tales to children as "Lady Amuck, Storyteller."

Her greatest thrill was having the opportunity to tell stories at Raffles Hotel in Singapore while living there in the mid '90's.

She has also taught expatriates drama outside of London, England.

Her certification is in elementary education and she has taught fourth grade and kindergarten.

Pam's written and published another book of humorous poetry titled <u>The Lives of the Wits and Famous.</u>

Children's stories and other poems have been published in <u>The Lincroft Journal</u> (NJ) and <u>The Public Pamphlet</u> (VA).

Humorous essays have appeared in <u>The American</u> (Surrey, England).

Dedication

This book is dedicated to the memory of my dear and longtime friend, Louise.

Acknowledgement

Love and thanks to Wayne for his patience and encouragement throughout this entire creative process.

TABLE OF CONTENTS

Chapter One

"Meet Hannah Savannah"

Hannah slipped out of the heavy, rain-pelted tent. She stood up, and stretched. Her ten-year old frame was lean and she was so happy to see the sun starting to peer from behind the powerful clouds that had been hanging over her brick row home off of Jones Street for over a week.

"WAHOO!"

Hannah started to do a series of cartwheels on the patio courtyard. It was neat that summer vacation had begun and she could once again have lots of fun time for herself.

Looking up, Hannah saw her younger brother, Nathan, looking out of a window and making faces at her. She returned the gesture.

Nathan. Would she have to baby sit him *again* this summer? Why didn't her older sister,

Christina, have to baby sit anymore? Just because she had a job out at the beach at Tybee, did not mean that she was not a big part of the Hunt family. Life was not fair!

"Hannah Savannah, come inside. I've made sweet tea. You ought to cool off a bit before we pick up Christina."

Hannah looked over to see her mother coming out onto the patio carrying more geranium plants.

"Mama, those are just heavenly," Hannah exclaimed. "I like that purple shade. I'd love a tee shirt that color! Can we go to the mall?"

Mrs. Hunt was a well-dressed woman in her early forties, and Hannah thought that she was the most beautiful person on the face of the earth.

Mama worked for a real estate company in downtown Savannah and Hannah was so very proud of her. She had sold quite a few homes in the two years that she had been working.

"Sweet thing, mind your mama now and go wash up," Mama answered. "Gracious, you ruin just about every nice thing that I buy for you. Look at those hands, Hannah!"

Hannah had always been the tomboy in her family.

She loved to be on the go and was extremely good in math at school. She had won the math bee two years in a row.

Toby McGillis had almost beaten her this past spring, but Hannah just knew that she was better at word problems.

It made her feel good to beat a boy…especially Toby 'Know-it-all' McGillis!

Hannah had the awards in frames over her bed. She was certain that a third award would be up there this year too.

Hannah's golden hair was tied up with two rubber bands most of the time, and everyone in town knew the energetic "Hannah Savannah!"

In fact, it was Hannah's grandfather, Grampy Levine, who had given her that name when she was only four years old.

Grampy lived in Ardsley Park in a big brick house that had a wooden swing set in the back yard.

He had been in the furniture business for many years and was a super duper artist and carpenter. Hannah liked to sit in the big kitchen with Grampy watching him draw funny cartoons.

He also made the best Gooey Fudge and Cheeserino Popcorn that Hannah had ever tasted. Delish and scrumptious! Nobody could make junk food as well as Grampy Levine. No siree.

Hannah had a superspendous idea! She and Christina would make him their famous Chocolate Pecan and Peanut Chocolate Chip Brownies again.

Hannah just hoped that Grampy would remember to take his teeth out of that glass he kept in his upstairs bathroom!

Chapter 2

"Pizza At Tybee"

"Your Daddy has to work with Mr. Sullivan this evening, so let's have pizza tonight," Mama suggested as she drove into a parking lot near the beach later that afternoon.

Hannah and Nathan were sitting in the back seat while Christina slid into the front seat with her mother.

"I had lots of visitors in the store today, Mother," she remarked. "I met a really nice guy too. He's from Atlanta and he's a park ranger."

"Not to mention that he's handsome, rich, and so very smart." laughed Mama.

Pulling down the mirror from the sun visor, Christina grinned while putting on her lipstick and blush. "I think he likes me too."

Hannah made a face. "Don't you get tired of putting that sticky stuff all over your face Chrissie? Doesn't it just sweat off anyway?"

Hannah knew that she *never* wanted to use all of the creams, powders, and sticky tubes that her sister kept in their bathroom. There wasn't any room on the counter and that drove Hannah Savannah bananas!

At least Eduardo Cortes, Hannah's first best friend, did not like goo all over girls' faces.

Eduardo lived on the east side of Forsyth Park and was new to Savannah. He was also going into the fifth grade.

His family came from Costa Rica. All that Hannah knew about Costa Rica was that it was as sticky and as hot as Savannah and was stuck somewhere below The United States on a map.

Eduardo's daddy was some kind of doctor who fixed up wrinkles and stuff on ladies' faces and other places. It was too disgusting for Hannah to even think about. Yuck.

Hannah decided that she had better phone Eduardo tonight with plans for tomorrow's adventures.

Christina looked at Hannah once they were all inside the pizza shop.

"You should use a little blush, Hannah. You're way too pale. I'll show you how to put it on if you want me to."

Hannah rolled her big green eyes. "Nope. Not me. I'm never gonna put that gunk on my face."

Christina laughed at her sister. "Once you get a boyfriend you will."

"No way," Hannah said.

Hannah was not interested in boys except for Eduardo. He wasn't a park ranger or really handsome. He had two teeth that kind of stuck out when he laughed and he was always tripping over his sneakers because he never tied his laces.

Hannah wished that she could get him away from his dumb old computer. He was always up in his room playing games on it.

Computers were boring to Hannah. They reminded her of school. It was boring too.

"The only reason you're so tan is because you work here on the beach. When I get a job, I'll work down by the river. I might want to work on a shrimp boat even," Hannah said.

Christina made a face. "Shrimp boats? Just don't you dare come near me afterwards! P. U!"

Mama laughed. "Just keep on using sun screen…especially you, Hannah."

Hannah Savannah had so many freckles that her Daddy often joked that he needed a magic marker to "connect the dots!"

Hannah didn't care. Freckles were supposed to be "love kisses from angels." Lots of folks told her that.

Little Nathan reached over, unscrewed the cap on the cheese, and poured the entire jar all over the pie.

"Nathan!"

Mama frowned. " Don't you ever do that again. We can help ourselves to the cheese, little man."

She then picked up a knife and spread the cheese across the pizza.

"Nathan, you've ruined the whole pie now," complained Christina glaring at her four-year-old brother.

Hannah just grinned. "I *love* it with lots of cheese. Way to go, Nathan!"

Grampy's popcorn

Yum!

↑ Gooey Fudge

Chapter 3

"A Key Is Missing!"

*"Boomalee, gloomalee, zoomalee whee
Eduardo is IT but he won't catch me!"*

Hannah Savannah ran around the courtyard in frenzy.

Eduardo Cortes chased his best friend around Mama's colorful geranium, marigold and petunia garden and then back up the wrought iron stairs.

His large brown eyes were wide with anticipation of tagging Hannah, but as usual, she had outrun him.

"Come on, Drooley!" ordered Hannah.

The Basset Hound waddled along, drooling at the mouth. That's how he got his name.

Mama had once tied a humongous yellow bandana around his neck to catch his slobber but that hadn't helped much.

Hannah thought Drooley was kind of dumb and disgusting sometimes, but she loved him just the same.

Eduardo, wearing a green velvet cape and a hat with feathers on it, quickly slid down the banister.

"I remember when you wore that to the Halloween fest," Hannah remarked, beginning to get out of breath now.

"I knew you would win first place, cause your mama sure can sew," she continued.

Eduardo smiled at his friend.

Drooley! Get your nose out of Mama's garden this instant!" shouted Hannah.

Drooley was making a path through Mama's prized flowerbed.

He dropped a big bone and then plopped down right into the middle of the brightly colored flowers.

"Drooley! Bad dog! Get outta Mama's garden now!"

Drooley just grunted and put his big black and tan head down to take a nap.

Hannah put her hands on her hips and frowned. Drooley always listened to her.

What was wrong with him?

Now Mama's flowers were squished!

Hannah reached down to tug at the big dog, but she couldn't get him to budge.

"Drooley Jasper Aloysius Hunt! You're not going to the park with me if you don't get outta there right now!"

Hannah was wearing a bright purple tee shirt. Mama had taken her to the mall over the weekend. There had been a sale…three tees for ten dollars!

Nathan had gotten a tee too, but he had spilled chocolate milk all over it. He cried and whined a whole lot and had embarrassed Hannah.

His screams were the worst she had ever heard in her entire life. A little guy Nathan's size just couldn't have lungs that big. Could he?

Eduardo grinned and suddenly reached out to tag Hannah. "Too bad, Hannah Savannah. You're IT now! Gotcha!"

Hannah shrugged. "I'm tired anyway."

She stretched out on the brick near Drooley's head and stared up at the sun starting to set in the sky. "Wanna star gaze tonight when Daddy puts the tent up? I can see The Big Dipper sometimes, you know."

Eduardo had been invited to sleep over for "Tent Night."

Tent Nights were Hannah Savannah's favorite activity during summer break. Besides, she didn't have to share a room with Chrissie and all of Chrissie's junk!

Tiesha Arbogast had also been invited. She was Hannah's second best friend.

Tiesha's mama and daddy were divorced. Hannah just couldn't imagine how that felt. However, Tiesha always seemed happy and had told her friend that it was kind of neat having two houses to live in.

"Besides, both mama and daddy love me to pieces," Tiesha added.

Tiesha's mama was a very beautiful and famous African-American model who now lived in a humongous apartment in New York.

She was way too skinny and needed more meat on her bones, thought Hannah (Grampy would say the same thing to Hannah when she would not eat).

Tiesha and her sister, Vonda, stayed with their daddy, but they would visit and travel with their mama during holidays.

Hannah hoped that she could visit New York City one day with Tiesha.

Tiesha loved it when Hannah Savannah would invite her over for Tent Night cause Hannah knew good games and fun stuff to do. Nobody ever got bored.

The back door suddenly swung open and Hannah's Mama appeared with a very pretty woman in a red summer dress.

The lady had a nice smile and gigantic pearls around her neck.

Hannah thought about Grams Levine and the pearls she had always worn.

Grams had died "peacefully" everyone had said. But it didn't matter to Hannah if Grams was dead in peace or not. All Hannah knew was that Grampy was lonely and that everyone missed Grams a whole lot.

"Hannah and Eduardo, this is Mrs. Kelly. She wants to rent our carriage house. The problem is that I can't find the key," Mama explained worriedly. "Daddy can't find the key that he had either."

Suddenly, Mama's mouth flew open in horror. "Oh dear me. Drooley is ruining my flowers!"

Drooley groaned and slowly got up and trudged out of the garden. His head was down in shame. He *knew* when Mama was mad!

"How do you do," Hannah said, holding out her hand to shake the pretty woman's hand. Mama had told Hannah that this was the polite way of saying 'Hey' to people.

"This is my best friend, Eduardo," Hannah said.

The lady smiled but kept glancing at her watch.

Eduardo looked down at his shoes and smiled. Eduardo could be so shy at times.

"It's a long gold key, Hannah. It was in a little red case. I just know I had it this morning before I planted flowers. I've looked all over the place for it," Mama said.

Hannah grinned. "Eduardo and I are spies. If we get Tiesha to help us, maybe we can solve this mystery for you Mama."

Mama sighed. "You just need to look for me, that's all, Hannah. Daddy will be home soon to put up your tent. Could you and Eduardo please keep an eye on Nathan for a minute while I try to see if we can get any of the windows to move for us?"

Hannah knew that her Mama was really stressed out now.

Mama and the lady walked to the back carriage house.

Hannah and Eduardo bounded up the stairs and into the house.

Drooley followed… huffing, puffing, and slobbering.

Chapter 4

"A Ghost!"

"Look at that moon!" whispered Tiesha, peering up into the night sky from her sleeping bag. "It has a creepy face on it!"

Hannah and Eduardo were busily munching handfuls of snacks.

Hannah shook her head. "I know something that is creepier than that moon, Tiesha."

Eduardo looked up. "It doesn't have a face, Tiesha. It doesn't look creepy to me."

"Does too," retorted Tiesha, reaching into a bag of chips.

Hannah unzipped her sleeping bag, stood up, and beamed her flashlight up at a building that overlooked the terrace.

"Eduardo and I saw a ghost up there one day, Tiesha. Honest over my heart! It was right in the front window of that building. Remember Eduardo?"

Eduardo nodded. "We saw a ghost of some old lady, Tiesha."

Tiesha sat up and crossed her arms. "Y'all making fun of me now. There aren't any ghosts. Papa told me that and you can't scare me."

Tiesha's daddy was a music teacher at the high school. He also played the saxophone and made the most beautiful music that Hannah had ever heard.

Daddy, Mama, and Hannah often walked to his jazz concerts down on the riverfront. Afterwards, Hannah got to sleep over with Tiesha. They would stay up most of the night and just giggle and eat ham sandwiches with lots of butter.

Hannah knew that Tiesha would become an artist one day. She was really good at origami and all kinds of paper cutting. She won many of the their school's art contests.

Tiesha had even cut Nathan a row of paper soldiers last Christmas. It was pretty awesome.

Hannah had tried to learn but was not as good or as fast of a folder and cutter as Tiesha. But then again, Tiesha Arbogast could never be as good a spy as Hannah Savannah!

Hannah always kept a journal when she would find something mysterious going on downtown.

She and Eduardo took notes when one of the sweet stores had a break-in and was robbed of chocolate candy and four Key Lime pies. Key Lime was Hannah's favorite pie in the whole wide world!

Hannah knew that stealing wasn't nice, but somehow she just could not imagine a better crime. The robbers had not wanted any money…just something sweet!

Hannah told the owners of the shop that she and Eduardo would get on the case as soon as spring break ended. That seemed to make the owners feel better about being robbed.

Hannah now crept across the courtyard and beamed her flashlight higher.

"We swear on sawdust and cream cheese, Tiesha. A ghost face came right to the front window of that building and scared the heck out of us when we were walking Drooley. It *was* an old woman," Hannah insisted.

"Well there are lots of old ladies who live in buildings, Hannah. I spose you think this ghost stole your Mama's carriage house key too?" asked Tiesha, getting up to follow her friend.

"But you see, Tiesha, that building has been empty for a couple of years cause they are reverbfreshing…re…doing something to it," explained Hannah.

Eduardo stayed in his sleeping bag and watched both girls as they tried to shine the light into the windows of the very old building.

He hadn't thought of that! Maybe that ghost *had* stolen the key. Poor Mrs. Hunt. She'd never get that key back now.

All Eduardo knew was that he had seen an old lady ghost in a building behind Hannah's house. It had scared the bee jeepers out of him.

Tiesha

Eduardo

CHAPTER 5

"Good Old Drooley"

"You truly mustn't talk to strangers, Hannah," Mama and Daddy would often warn Hannah when she would take Drooley out for short walks onto Pulaski Square near her row home.

Well, that's easy for them to say, thought Hannah. Goodness to mergatroid! Didn't they realize that Savannah was swarming with tourists most of the year?

Hannah couldn't help the fact that she and Drooley were so popular with everyone.

Drooley loved to take walks, except when the weather was absolutely sticky, droopingly, sweltering hot… in which case, Hannah would bring along a jug of lemonade and two paper cups.

Drooley was the only pet Hannah knew that lapped up lemonade from a cup.

Sometimes the tourists would murmur

"Oh, how cute!" and take Hannah's and Drooley's picture.

Hannah kept looking in famous magazines to see if their pictures were there, but they never were.

Hannah and Drooley met a man and his wife walking three little poodles on one leash. They were from Paris. That's a humongous city in France across the Atlantic Ocean.

Hannah told the tourists that her big sister, Christina, knew how to cuss in French.

She also told them all about Grampy Levine and going to temple and to church.

"We're kind of a jumbly family," Hannah would explain. "My Mama and my Grampy are Jewish. My Daddy is sort of like a pilgrim. His kin come from Cape Cod. Someday, I am going visit my Grandma Hunt up north. She knows how to suck fish out of shells."

Hannah could not get over how she much she could make tourists laugh.

Hannah soon thought about "Daisy" when she saw a tall red-haired boy walking a Siamese cat on a leash across the square.

Drooley began to growl his silly growl and Hannah tugged at his leash.

Hannah's family had once had a cat named "Daisy."

It had been named after Juliette Gordon Low, the founder of the Girl Scouts.

Daisy had been Juliette Gordon Lowe's nickname. This famous woman had been born and raised in a house near Tiesha's, right off of Bull Street.

Girl Scouts galore were always walking about. Hannah and Tiesha liked to compare the badges that they had earned with the visiting Girl Scouts.

Mama and Daddy had spent up to two thousand dollars on a veterinarian's bill when Hannah was about five, because "Daisy," the cat, had eaten some kind of thread and it had gotten tangled in its innards. Mama had cried a lot and the operation had taken a long time.

All string, twine, and thread were put up high in the Hunts' cupboards from then on.

Grampy and Grams Levine had taken care of "Daisy" when Hannah and her daddy had picked up Drooley from the dog pound.

Poor old Drooley. Somebody had left him at a gas station on Montgomery Avenue. Hannah could not imagine anyone being so cruel to a poor helpless animal.

Daddy had seen Drooley's face in the newspaper. He told Mama that this was the dog he had always longed for.

Mama had told Daddy that "Daisy" was just the right pet for the Hunt family, and that she didn't think they needed an old mangy hound dog.

Hannah had been so happy Daddy had won that argument.

Chapter 6

"Captain Kidd-U-Knot"

"Ho yo yo and a bottle of milk!"

The group of children giggled as Captain Kidd-U-Knot patted his belly and made a gruff face.

He was wearing a red bandana designed with parrots, as well as blue denim pullover pants with a blue and white striped shirt.

A fishnet was hung over his shoulder. It had all kinds of plastic fish tangled in it.

His pirate hat was crooked and he had a red wig hanging out underneath it.

Hannah had never seen such an outfit and thought it might be perfect for Halloween.

No way, she then reminded herself. Hannah Savannah was a super spy and spies didn't wear silly pirate clothes.

Today was Nathan's fifth birthday.

Daddy had hired a storyteller pirate to entertain for the afternoon.

Mama had baked red, white, and blue cupcakes and was going to serve them with bubblegum ice cream, of course.

Nathan kept pointing to the stuffed parrot atop the pirate's shoulder.

Nathan loved birds. Hannah knew he would ask the pirate for the parrot before the party was over. Her little brother wanted everything that he laid his eyes upon.

Sometimes he would just downright embarrass Hannah. He was always putting his fingers up his nose. Hannah hoped that they would swell and just get stuck up there one day. Yuck.

Mama would try to shush him and Nathan would sort of calm down...unless it was near the ice cream store at Market Square.

If bubblegum flavored ice cream was offered, Nathan wanted it or he would howl his brains out! Hannah didn't mind when he threw a fit at Market

Square, though. That meant ice cream for everyone!

Nathan had invited six of his friends, and Hannah had invited Tiesha and Eduardo to the birthday bash.

Christina was working out at Tybee. She's *always* working, thought Hannah, wishing her big sister could see this crazy looking seaman.

Just then, the pirate pulled out a humongous lizard from one of his bags. It was yellow, orange, and purple. It was about as big as Nathan!

"Where did you get that big lizard, Mr.?" asked Nathan.

"Ho yo yo! This is a gecko that I found while traveling about Singapore," answered the pirate. "Singapore is across the Pacific and Indian Oceans, many miles from Savannah."

Eduardo raised his hand. "My aunts and uncles have lots of geckos in Costa Rica!"

"Right you are! Geckos live where it is oh so hot and humid. These little critters climb the walls and eat tiny fleas and bugs. They do a fine job of it as well!" boomed the pirate, grinning and showing a black tooth.

"I'm going to sing you a song about *this* gecko, he said."

Captain Kidd-U-Knot then thrust the stuffed gecko sideways and held out its long tail.

The children started to giggle again.

"Hey, you have a gecko guitar!" shouted Nathan, scrambling up closer to the pirate.

"Indeed I do, young sailor!" exclaimed the pirate.

The group scurried up close to the pirate with the gecko guitar...

There's a gecko on my toothbrush
And I don't know what to do...
There's a gecko on my toothbrush
Should I send it to the zoo?
It is so squiggly-wiggly
With eyes bright as can be

If I try to put it into a cage
Do you think it'll be mad at me?

My Mom says it really is friendly
It eats ants and little fleas
Perhaps I can teach it manners...
Like "No thank you" and "please."
I think I'll just let it climb my walls
And live inside my home
But PLEASE don't eat my toothpaste
And leave my brush alone!

"Now it's your turn!" boomed the pirate.

Before long, the entire birthday party and Mama and Daddy were singing along with the funny looking pirate and his super sized gecko.

Hannah thought this was great fun and she was glad that her brother had just turned five.

She knew she would be even happier when Nathan turned ten!

...turning 5
today

Nathan's
Birthday
Party

Chapter 7

"Nobody Ever Believes Me"

Mama was about to call the locksmith.

The pretty lady who wanted to rent the carriage house was coming back to take a look at it.

Hannah begged Mama not to call the locksmith.

"Eduardo and I will find that key for you. We're super spies. Remember when I found Mr. Needham's glasses at school? He had me over for homemade ice cream. I wish Mr. Needham would lose something again," sighed Hannah.

Mama smiled as she looked through the yellow pages.

"Hannah dear, I need a key right away. I know you're the best spy on this very planet, but the locksmith will make me brand new keys."

Hannah frowned. "That old lady ghost took your key. I just know it!"

Mama put the phone book down and put her arms about her daughter.

" 'Elderly' sounds much nicer, Hannah."

"Well she looked pretty old to me, Mama. Eduardo is scared to look up into that window. I'm not. Spies aren't supposed to be afraid."

"And it is not nice looking into folks' windows either, young lady!"

Hannah pulled away and looked up into her Mama's big brown eyes.

"But if nobody lives over there, then how come we saw that old... elderly... lady looking down at us? She looked just like a ghost...all covered in white...she *had* to be a ghost!"

"Hannah Savannah, you have the most vivid imagination that I've ever come across in my lifetime!" said Mama. "It was probably a light of some kind that you saw."

"It was an old elderly lady ghost," Hannah insisted.

"Well Hannah, if you happen to talk to that ghost lady, please mention that your Mama is a real estate agent. I certainly hope she's paying her rent!" Mama laughed.

Hannah sulked over to the fridge. Mama sometimes just didn't understand. She would be thanking Hannah soon enough, though. Hannah would get that key back somehow.

All of Savannah would know about Hannah Savannah Super Spy. Yesiree, Hannah would be famous.

"I love you lots, sweet thing," Mama reminded her daughter.

Chapter 8

"You're Chicken Scared!"

Eduardo followed Hannah closely. The tall building had several trucks parked in front of it.

"Do you see the ghost lady up there Hannah?"

Hannah stood up on her tiptoes and peered as best she could up into the windows of the building.

"That window's too high. I can't see anything."

She pulled a large magnifying glass that Grampy Levine had given her out of her backpack.

Grampy had told her that she would not be a true spy unless she used this special "spy glass."

"Can I look into that Hannah?" Eduardo asked. "Maybe I'll see something that you don't. I'm a little taller than you, Hannah."

Eduardo reached up high on the toes of his sneakers. His laces were untied *again*.

Hannah wondered just how he could skateboard without tripping all over the place?

Hannah just glared at Eduardo. "No you're not. Your shoes just have more rubber on them. Sandals don't make me as tall cause they're flatter."

Eduardo reached down and slipped out his backpack bottle.

"I'm glad we're here while its daytime," he said, taking a long, cool drink.

"You're chicken scared at night," Hannah reminded her friend.

Eduardo made a face. "I am *not* scared."

"Yep. You are."

"Am not."

"Are too!"

"I'm not supposed to go to buildings at night, that's all. You aren't allowed either, Hannah."

Hannah shrugged and put the spyglass back into her bag.

She then wiped her face and shook her head. "I told Mama that we would get her key back but I forget which window that ghost lady's in."

Suddenly loud drilling began and both Hannah and Eduardo put their hands over their ears.

"I can't remember either," shouted Eduardo. "We can go back to your courtyard and play games if you feel like it."

"I spose so," sighed Hannah.

Hannah was not happy. This was the day that she had promised herself that she would find the gold key that her mother had been looking for. She was tired of playing dumb old games. She wanted to do something *exciting*!

Hannah had not been inside the old carriage house in quite a while…not since Mama had fixed it up. Maybe she and Eduardo could figure out a way to get into it.

Mama had kept it locked until she could find somebody to rent it. Now, Hannah was curious concerning how it looked inside.

I am *not* a very good spy today, Hannah groaned to herself.

Hannah and Drooley

Chapter 9

"Hurrah!"

Christina had the day off from work and was sunning herself in the courtyard when Hannah and Eduardo appeared.

She looks so like Mama in that bathing suit, thought Hannah as she shut the back door leading from the alleyway.

Christina and Mama had the same long dark brown hair. It was curly too.

Hannah and Nathan's hair was poker straight. You both are Daddy's side of the family as far as hair goes, Mama had once told Hannah.

Grandma Hunt was supposed to have had poker straight red hair when she was younger. Her hair was probably all white now.

Christina turned her head towards her younger sister. "It's my day off Hannah. Maybe y'all can play inside."

Hannah made a face. "It's my yard too."

Christina suddenly sat up." Nick's coming over this afternoon. We don't want to be bothered."

"Drooley's going to slobber all over your precious Nick," Hannah retorted.

Drooley kept scratching away at his bone near the flower garden.

Hannah ignored the dog. Christina could take care of the dumb dog for a change.

Christina looked her sister. "What's the matter Hannah?"

Hannah kicked at one of the bricks surrounding Mama's garden.

"We can't find that old ghost lady. I want to find Mama's key for her before she has to call in that man for new locks."

Christina giggled. "An old ghost lady? Hannah Savannah, you're a stitch!"

Hannah made a face. Goodness to mergatroid! Her sister now sounded just like Mama.

"We believe in ghosts and we saw one. If you don't believe us, then too bad."

Eduardo agreed. "It was another Savannah ghost, Chrissie. Honest."

"If y'all say so," said Christina.

Christina noticed Drooley pawing his way into the dirt and scattering it.

"Drooley, you're not being a good boy today at all! Hannah, you and Eduardo are sweaty. Could you both please move that dirt back into the flower garden?"

Hannah looked at her sister. "Why should we do anything for you when you laugh at us?"

"Okay," Christina said, rolling her brown eyes. "You *did* see a ghost."

Hannah and Eduardo plopped down next to Drooley who was panting and slobbering. "Drooley, you are such a pain," complained Hannah.

Both Hannah and Eduardo started to scoop up the dirt that was lying all over the brick.

"Drooley squishes Mama's flowers all of the time. Look, here's your dumb old bone," Hannah told the dog, dropping the yucky slobbery bone back down in front of him.

Drooley's going to obedience school one day when I get rich from spying, Hannah thought to herself. It's time this smelly dog learns some manners!

"Nathan is staying with Grampy so Mother can show houses. You'll have to stay put until she gets home," said Christina. "Daddy's just across the street helping Miss Adeline."

Christina was combing her darn hair again, trying to look glamorous. "Nick's taking me to the beach," she added.

Hannah got tired of Chrissie not being the sister that she had once known...the one who liked to roller skate fast down Grampy Levine's driveway...the sister who braided Hannah's hair for her anytime she wanted her to...the sister who would lick the beaters with Hannah every time they made Gooey Fudge.

How come sisters had to change and become weird?

Hannah frowned. "I never get to go to the beach anymore. Since Eduardo and I are doing you a good deed, can't you just take us too?"

"Noooo...I don't think so."

Christina put her sunglasses on top of her head. Nick's coming to see *me*. I'll take you both another time."

"Nick's never even met us," Hannah said, digging her nails further into the dirt around the flowerbed. "We promise not to bother you. We'll just walk out to the pier and watch the fishermen."

Eduardo let Drooley lick his face.

"Drooley, you smell soda pop on me, doncha boy? We went to the lake a couple of weeks ago, Hannah. It was so much fun," said Eduardo.

"I hate lakes. My toes get all squishy and caught in the mud and rocks," Hannah replied, pushing the mounds of dirt back into place.

As soon as Hannah had uttered these words, she felt something scrape the brick patio underneath her fingers.

"I FOUND IT! It's Mama's gold key to the carriage house, Eduardo! It was right here under the dirt."

Hannah quickly scrambled to her feet and held out the long gold key in her dirty hand so that Eduardo could see it.

All three of them stared at Drooley. He must have found the key and hidden it with his bone in the flowerbed!

"Good Drooley!" cried Hannah, leaning down to hug her most favorite dog in the whole wide world.

CHAPTER 10

"Case Closed"

"I just love shaved ice," shouted Hannah to Tiesha as they walked along River Street. Jazz musicians were beginning to play on a corner.

"Mine is grape and it's the best," Tiesha replied.

"No way. My lime is delish!"

Hannah and Tiesha were waiting for Daddy and Nathan to come out of one of the shops.

It was Arts On The River Weekend and brightly colored canopies were flapping in the summer breeze while vendors were setting up their crafts and merchandise.

Hannah loved to walk along the riverfront. It was probably her very favorite spot in Savannah.

Daddy had promised to take them all out to lunch. Mama was going to join them if she didn't have to show any more houses.

"I want to see if Mama and Daddy will buy me a spy outfit today, Tiesha. I think I need one, don't you?"

Tiesha shrugged. "What do spies wear?"

Hannah stopped to think. She was not sure.

"Maybe a raincoat?"

Tiesha laughed. "Lots of people wear raincoats."

"Well sometimes in the movies the spies wear raincoats," insisted Hannah.

"What do they wear then when the sun is out?" Tiesha asked.

Hannah shrugged.

"I think you should wear a big hat that's really different from other hats."

I don't like *straw* hats. Chrissie always wears one. It's stupid looking," said Hannah.

Tiesha agreed. "Maybe a hat with feathers then."

Hannah frowned. "Nah. Feathers make me allergic. Grams Levine had a dress with feathers on it. When I was a baby and she was holding me, Mama says I almost sneezed my entire brain out."

Tiesha giggled at her friend.

"I have a great idea! I'll make you a paper hat, Hannah."

Hannah thought for a moment, sipped the last of her shaved ice, and walked over to a trash bin.

"It needs to say HANNAH SAVANNAH SUPER SPY on it, Tiesha."

"Then it has to be one humongous hat. It'll take me a long time to print all that on it."

Hannah looked at her friend. "What'll I do if it rains? That hat will wilt for sure."

Tiesha frowned. She, too, hadn't thought about that.

Daddy and Nathan were coming out of the shop. Nathan had a bag in his hand. It was probably another toy boat. Hannah didn't care, as long as it kept him quiet.

Daddy pointed up the street. "Here comes Mama now. If you gals are finished, let's go and have some lunch."

Mama was wearing that green polka dot sundress that Daddy had bought her for their anniversary.

As she came closer, Hannah noticed that she also had on the big yellow paper mache flower pin that Hannah had made for her in school.

That darn old pin had taken Hannah so long to make in art class. She'd almost thrown it into the waste paper basket, but Mrs. Espy, the art teacher with the bug eyes, wouldn't have liked that at all. Hannah would have gotten yelled at for sure.

Mama smiled and looked right at Hannah. "Guess what I found out at work today, Hannah?"

Hannah did not know.

"One of the ladies that I work with has a mother who makes the insides of homes very pretty for people. She's called an interior decorator. Supposedly, she's been working in an apartment in the building that you've been spying on."

All eyes and ears were on Mama now.

"I think that you and Eduardo saw her hanging white curtains one day," Mama continued.

Hannah's mouth dropped. "But nobody lives in that building, Mama."

Mama smiled. "But that doesn't mean that workers aren't fixing it up on the inside."

Tiesha leaned over and whispered into her best friend's ear. "I'm *still* going to make you that hat, Hannah."

Walking along the cobblestone pavement, Mama made an announcement.

"Just think, everyone," she said. "If I didn't have Hannah Savannah Super Spy as a daughter, then I wouldn't now have the key to the carriage house."

Daddy agreed. "We're able to rent it because of you, kiddo. Great work!"

Hannah smiled to herself. She couldn't wait for Tiesha to get started on that super spy hat.

TheEnd

River Street

Appendix

Hannah Savannah And Friends Recipes

These recipes have been tasted and shared with many.
Enjoy them!

Grampy Levine's Gooey Fudge

2 (6 oz.) pkg. chocolate chips

1 can of Eagle Brand condensed milk

2 tbsp. margarine

1 (10 1/2 oz.) pkg. mini marshmallows

In saucepan, melt chocolate, margarine and milk.

In large bowl, mix all with marshmallows
Spread onto wax paper lined 13 x 9 inch pan.
Chill 2 hours.

Hannah and Christina's Wahoo Brownies

1/2 cup of butter

2 large eggs

1 cup of flour sifted

1 tsp of vanilla

1 cup of chocolate chips

½ cup of packed light brown sugar

¼ cup of peanut butter

¼ cup of pecans and ¼ cup of peanuts

Preheat oven to 350 degrees. Grease 8x8 inch pan. Combine butter, peanut butter, and chocolate chips in saucepan on low heat. Stir often until melted.

Beat eggs in mixing bowl. Add sugar and vanilla. Beat to mix. Add chocolate mixture and stir.

Add flour and nuts. Stir until well mixed. Scrape batter into pan. Bake in oven for 25 minutes. Cool brownies before cutting.

Cheeserino Popcorn!

Pop any brand of microwave popcorn

Please do not burn

Pour contents into large bowl

Add a sprinkle of garlic powder

Thoroughly sprinkle grated Romano and
Parmesan cheese onto the popcorn.

Stir well

Enjoy with sweet tea or soft drinks.

Watch a good movie with family or
friends

Señora Corte's Lime/Apple Delight Salad

1 small jar of applesauce

1 cup boiling water

1 package lime Jell-O

½ cup cold water

1/3 cup chopped macadamia nuts

Dissolve Jell-O in hot water. Add cold water, applesauce, and nuts.
Mix and let chill in square pan.
When it sets, cut into squares. Serve on lettuce leaves.
This is a delish salad with any Spanish food!

Tiesha's Soup

4 cups chicken broth
1 jalapeno pepper, seeded
1/2 cup crunchy peanut butter
1/2 cup minced green bell pepper
1/2 cup chopped onion

In 1-quart saucepan add broth and chili pepper and bring mixture to a boil. Stir in bell pepper and onion and return to a boil. Reduce heat to low, cover, and let simmer until vegetables are tender, about 10 minutes.

Reduce heat to lowest possible temperature. Then add peanut butter and cook, stirring constantly, until peanut butter is melted and mixture is well blended.